VICTORY ★ SCHOOL SUPERSTARS

9-H

Sports Illustrated KIDS

STONE ARCH BOOKS
a capstone imprint

It's Hard to Dribble with Your Feet

by Val Priebe

illustrated by Jorge Santillan

STONE ARCH BOOKS
a capstone imprint

VICTORY SCHOOL SUPERSTARS

Sports Illustrated KIDS *It's Hard to Dribble With Your Feet*
is published by Stone Arch Books — A Capstone Imprint
151 Good Counsel Drive, P.O. Box 669
Mankato, Minnesota 56002
www.capstonepub.com

Art Director and Designer: Bob Lentz
Creative Director: Heather Kindseth
Production Specialist: Michelle Biedscheid

Photo credits: Shutterstock/billyhoiler (bottom left),
sjgh (top left), Eric Isselée (top right); Sports Illustrated/
Jerry Cooke (middle left), Peter Read Miller (bottom right).

Library of Congress Cataloging-in-Publication Data is
available on the Library of Congress website.

ISBN: 978-1-4342-2016-5 (library binding)
ISBN: 978-1-4342-2782-9 (paperback)

Summary: When Carmen, a basketball star, joins the soccer
team, she struggles to learn the new sport.

Printed in the United States of America in Stevens Point, Wisconsin.
032010   005741WZF10

TABLE of CONTENTS

CHAPTER 1
A New Sport..................... 6

CHAPTER 2
Asking Dad..................... 16

CHAPTER 3
My First Day..................... 22

CHAPTER 4
Not Good Enough?............... 28

CHAPTER 5
Hard Work..................... 38

CHAPTER 6
Our First Game.................. 42

CARMEN SKORE

AGE: 10   **SPORTS:** Basketball, Soccer

SUPER SPORTS ABILITY: Super dribbling makes Carmen a basketball star.

VICTORY

A New Sport

It's lunchtime at the Victory School for Super Athletes. All around me are kids with amazing abilities.

I spot my friend Alicia carrying her tray. Alicia is a cheerleader who can jump a hundred feet in the air. She's trying to get around a group of kids who aren't moving an inch. So what does she do? She just jumps over them!

I'm sitting with my friends, Josh and Tyler. Josh is a super skater. When he's on the ice, his feet don't falter. Tyler plays basketball. He is the team's best shooter. He never misses!

I play basketball, too. I'm known for my super dribbling skills. I can keep total control of the ball, no matter what.

As I eat with my right hand, I like to dribble my basketball with my left hand. I figure there is no harm. The ball will never get away from me, and I mean never.

Josh and Tyler are talking about some TV show. For some reason, my dad doesn't think we need a TV. So I don't have much to say. I quit paying attention and let myself space out.

But suddenly, I hear my name and jump.

"Earth to Carmen!" Josh says. "Did you even hear me?"

"No, sorry. Thanks to my dad, I have nothing to say when the subject of TV comes up," I say.

"We asked if you were going to go out for a fall sport," Tyler says.

"Since basketball won't start for a few months," Josh adds.

"She's going to try out for soccer," says a voice behind me. It is my best friend, Lynsey. She sits down with us.

"I am?" I ask. The only time I've ever played soccer was in gym class. I have never thought about joining the team.

"It is so much fun. And wouldn't it be cool to be teammates?" asks Lynsey.

Lynsey has been playing soccer since she was three. She was always good. But when she turned eight, she discovered her super skill, kicking. At almost every game, she kicks the ball into the goal from the opposite side of the field. You have to see it to believe it.

"Plus, it's fun to try a new sport," says Josh with a grin. Josh is a figure skater, but he recently tried out for the hockey team.

"Being on a team together *would* be fun," I say to Lynsey. "But I have to ask my dad before I can join."

"Ask tonight!" says Lynsey.

I am still not sure I will be any good at soccer. But I like trying new things. And I love hanging out with Lynsey.

"All right, you got it!" I say.

Asking Dad

After dinner, I sit down at the table to do my homework. My dad is washing the dishes.

"Dad?" I ask.

"Yeah," says Dad.

"Can I join the soccer team?" I ask.

Dad dries his hands, turns around, and looks at me. "Sure you can join soccer," he says. "What made you decide that?"

"Lynsey mentioned it at lunch," I say. "It sounds like a lot of fun."

"Well, I know how much you like trying new things," says Dad.

"Thanks, Dad!" I say. I give him a big hug. "I have to go call Lynsey!"

I look up at Dad and see that his eyebrows are raised. "After I finish my homework?" I add. Dad smiles again.

"After you finish your homework," he agrees.

As soon as I'm done, I race to my room to call Lynsey.

"We are going to have so much fun!" she squeals. I can tell she is smiling.

"See you tomorrow," I say.

As I hang up, I start to worry. What if I'm not any good? I can dribble a basketball better than almost anyone. But how can that help with soccer?

Before I can worry too much, I get ready for bed. As I fall asleep, I feel excited about trying something new.

My First Day

A week later, I am officially a Victory soccer player. Lynsey has been talking about soccer nonstop. I don't say much. I just don't know much about soccer. And I feel nervous when I think about it too much.

It's time to get ready for practice. I head into the locker room and change into my shorts and T-shirt. I tighten the laces on my new shoes. The lady at the store called them cleats. They have funny little knobs on the bottoms for running in the grass.

"Aren't you excited, Carmen?" asks Lynsey as she puts her hair into a ponytail.

"I am more nervous than excited," I say.

"Don't worry. You are going to be great! Now let's get out there," says Lynsey.

We walk to the field behind the school. Some other girls are already kicking soccer balls around. Our coach, Coach Claire, introduces herself, and we get to work.

We run a couple of laps and stretch out. I start to relax. After all, this is a lot like basketball. Then we each get a soccer ball and practice dribbling. This is *not* like basketball.

We are supposed to move the ball back and forth between our feet. At the same time, we run down the field. Lynsey is so much better than I am.

I can't go very fast, and the ball keeps getting away from me. One of the other girls laughs as my ball rolls behind me.

At the end of practice, I have a lot of doubts. It's hard to dribble with your feet!

What if I'm not good enough to play? What if I don't learn fast enough? What if Lynsey wishes she had never asked me to play?

Not Good Enough?

I might be worried about soccer, but
I am no quitter. I need to practice, and
I have a lot of questions for Lynsey. I'm
sure I can be good at any sport that
has dribbling.

"Why do you have to dribble?" I ask Lynsey between classes the next day. "How long does it take to learn?"

Lynsey explains, "Dribbling helps keep the ball away from the other team. It's really hard to steal the ball away from a good dribbler."

"Just like in basketball," I say. "Too bad my super dribbling skills don't carry over to soccer."

"You'll get better, Carmen," says Lynsey. "By the end of the season, you will be great, just like you are at basketball."

"I don't think so. In basketball, I have something special. I have something no one else has. In soccer, I'm just normal," I say.

"You don't have a super shooting skill in basketball, right?" asks Lynsey.

"Right," I say.

"But you still score around ten points a game. How do you do that?" she asks.

"I practice," I say.

"Right, so what do you think you need to do to improve at soccer?" asks Lynsey.

"All right, I know what you are getting at," I say.

"Then say it," she says.

"I need to practice," I say, smiling.

* * *

As the last bell of the day rings, I hurry to the locker room. I am eager to start practicing. I always work to be the best I can at everything I try.

I pull out my practice gear in the locker room. At the other end of the bench, two of my teammates are changing.

Suddenly, I hear one of them say, "I don't know why they let new people join teams, anyway. It's not like we came to Victory to try new sports." The other girl is saying something back, but I can't catch it.

Their voices fade as they walk out of the locker room. I wait until they are long gone before I shut my locker. Then I slowly walk to the second day of practice.

I try not to let what I heard bother me.
After all, things at Victory are different
than at other schools. Everyone has their
sport, something that they are really great
at. I tell myself that I will not give up. I just
have to work extra hard.

We have two weeks of practice before our first game. I will use every spare minute I have to work on dribbling.

CHAPTER 5

Hard Work

For two weeks I have had nothing but soccer on the brain. I have practiced dribbling and passing and shooting. I do all those things in basketball, of course. But with a soccer ball, it is completely different.

I practiced on my own, and I practiced with Lynsey. We even had a sleepover and played in my backyard until it was too dark to see. I might not be great yet, but I am definitely getting better.

It is the night before our first game. I tried to eat dinner earlier, but it was hard. My stomach is filled with butterflies.

I haven't heard the girls from the locker room talk about me again, but I can't forget what they said. I really want to show everyone that I deserve to be part of the Victory soccer team.

Sure, I have had a hard time changing my super basketball dribbling skills into super soccer dribbling skills. But the more I work, the easier it is getting.

I've done all I can before this first game. Now the only thing left to do is get some rest. I fall asleep imagining how great it would feel to do a good job tomorrow.

CHAPTER 6

Our First Game

The school day has been a total blur. It is hard to focus on schoolwork with the game just around the corner.

After school, I meet Lynsey in the locker room. We head out to the soccer field for warm-ups.

"Here we go. It's game time!" shouts Lynsey as she runs out to play. She is a starting player. I settle onto the bench to cheer on the team.

Lynsey is so fun to watch. The whole crowd cheers when she scores a goal from the kick off. The ball easily soars more than sixty feet to land in the goal.

In the final quarter of the game, Coach Claire calls me over.

"Carmen, I want you to go in for Anna," she says.

"But it is so close. We are just one goal behind," I say.

"I know how to keep score, Carmen. And I know I want you out there. Get going!" says Coach Claire.

"Yes, ma'am," I say.

I take a deep breath and run onto the field. Now is not the time to think about being nervous or good enough. Now is the time to play.

Now is the time to play . . . that's it! Soccer is just a game, like basketball. All I have to do is play it.

Just a few seconds later, I hear Lynsey yell, "Carmen!"

She passes me the ball. I dribble as best I can. I even keep the ball away from the girl who is guarding me. As soon as I am close enough, I kick the ball hard. It soars into the goal just as the buzzer sounds!

I just scored the tying goal, and we are going into overtime! Lynsey grabs my arms and starts jumping up and down. Then a girl that I have never talked to appears.

"Nice shot, Carmen," she says, giving me a high five. I recognize her. It is the girl from the locker room! "I'm sorry I ever doubted you," she says. "Welcome to the team!"

SUPERSTAR OF THE WEEK
Carmen Skore

Basketball star Carmen Skore took a chance and tried a new sport — soccer. She worked hard to learn the game. For that, she is our Superstar of the Week.

How does soccer compare to basketball?
Both games take a lot of energy, but basketball is a lot easier for me. Since I don't have a super skill in soccer, I felt really behind. It was so embarrassing. But when I started getting better, it felt so good.

What is your favorite class in school?
I love science. It is really cool when we do experiments! One time, we made this glowing green slime. It bounced when you threw it. We all started throwing it around the room, of course. Our teacher got super mad!

What do you do when you aren't playing sports?
Me and my BFF, Lynsey, hang out whenever we can. We play video games at her house or look at magazines at mine.

What is your favorite type of ice cream?
Mint chocolate chunk! Yum! But I only have it for special occasions.

GLOSSARY

abilities (uh-BIL-i-teez)—skills or powers

definitely (DEF-uh-nit-lee)—surely

dribbling (DRIB-uhl-ing)—moving the ball with gentle kicks while running

falter (FAWL-tur)—to pause or move in an unsteady way

introduces (in-truh-DOOSS-es)—helps someone meet a new person

mentioned (MEN-shuhnd)—spoke about something briefly

officially (uh-FISH-uhl-ee)—with approval from someone in charge

recognize (REK-uhg-nize)—to see or hear someone and know who the person is

SOCCER IN HISTORY

 A game similar to soccer is played in China.

1500 B.C. A game similar to soccer is played in China.

1863 A.D. Soccer clubs in **England** make rules for the game. Before these rules, players could bite, kick, and punch each other.

1904 Seven countries form the FIFA soccer association in Europe. Today there are 208 FIFA members.

1930 The first World Cup is played. This tournament is played every four years. Today, more than five billion people watch the final match on TV.

1966 The World Cup trophy is stolen in London. A **dog** named Pickles finds it a week later.

1975 **Pelé** moves to the United States from Brazil. He is one of the greatest players of all time.

1991 The first Women's World Cup is played. The United States beats Norway to win.

1999 The **United States** wins its second Women's World Cup.

2010 **South Africa** hosts the World Cup. This is the first time it is held in Africa.

ABOUT THE AUTHOR

VAL PRIEBE

Val Priebe lives in St. Paul, Minnesota, with four dogs, a cat named Cowboy, and a guy named Nick. Besides writing books, she loves to spend her time reading, knitting, cooking, and coaching basketball. Val has also written several books in the popular Jake Maddox series, including *Full Court Dreams* and *Stolen Bases*.

ABOUT THE ILLUSTRATOR

JORGE SANTILLAN

Jorge Santillan got his start illustrating in the children's sections of local newspapers. He opened his own illustration studio in 2005. His creative team specializes in books, comics, and children magazines. Jorge lives in Mendoza, Argentina, with his wife, Bety, and their four dogs, Fito, Caro, Angie, and Sammy.

VICTORY SCHOOL SUPERSTARS

Read them ALL!

STONE ARCH BOOKS
a capstone imprint